This book belongs to

_____

_____

For Ellie
D.C.

To Marko
D.K.

First published in Great Britain in 2008 by Gullane Children's Books
This paperback edition published in 2009 by
Gullane Children's Books
185 Fleet Street, London, EC4A 2HS
www.gullanebooks.com

3   5   7   9   10   8   6   4   2

Text © David Conway 2008
Illustrations © Dubravka Kolanovic 2008

The right of David Conway and Dubravka Kolanovic to be identified as the author and illustrator of this work has been asserted by them in accordance with the Copyright, Designs and Patents Act, 1988.

A CIP record for this title is available from the British Library.

ISBN: 978-1-86233-762-6

Printed and bound in China

The Secret to Teddy's Happiness

David Conway

illustrated by

Dubravka Kolanovic

GULLANE
CHILDREN'S BOOKS

One night, while all the house was sleeping, the toys in the playroom discovered an old abandoned bear that the children had found. Its fur was matted and its ears were worn. It looked like the most bedraggled and unhappy teddy bear that ever was.

The toys cleaned it up and found the bear some clothes.
They made a small bed out of whatever they could
find, and set it by the toy box in the playroom.

But despite all their efforts there was a problem. The shabby
old bear seemed just as sad as when they had found it.
"It's his heart," said the giraffe, "it's broken. That bear
needs more than clothes and a comfortable bed
to sleep in. It needs to feel happy again."

So that night as moonlight filled the whole room,
the toys embarked on a quest, to go and find the secret,
the secret to Teddy's happiness.

They caught a train,

and then a plane . . .

. . . and sailed on a carpet sea.

They searched the playroom and rummaged around.
But they could not find the secret. No secret could be found.

Then the friends encountered a rabbit who
knew everything there was to know, from the
height of the tallest building, to where
the snow goes when it's not winter.

But the little velvet rabbit had longed for
one thing since the day it was fashioned and sewn.
"I will tell you the secret," said the kind little rabbit,
"if you bring me a star of my own."

So the adventurous toys went in
search of a star in a rickety old toy car.

They found some hanging in the baby's room,
attached by strings to a luminous moon.
"I will give you a star," whispered the moon, "but then,
you must shine a light upon me so I can glimmer again."

So the brave little toys went in search of a light
as all the clocks in the house struck midnight . . .

They found one on an island by a shabby
old lion, but the lion wanted something in return.

"It is cold on this island," said the sleepy old lion, in a
slow and slumberous yawn. "But I will give you this light
if you bring me a scarf that will keep me nice and warm."

So the monkey, the robot,
the raccoon and the giraffe
set off in the moonlight
to search for a scarf . . .

. . . along the dark
murky hallway . . .

. . . down a mountain steep . . .

. . . where they found one piled up
with some coats in a heap.

Then the party of friends returned to the island
and wrapped the scarf around the lion's mane . . .

. . . they shone the light upon the luminous
moon to make it glow and glimmer again.

They flew to the bookshelf on a rocket ship
where the little velvet rabbit lived all alone . . .

. . . and presented it with a tiny star,
one it could call its own.

Then the rabbit revealed the secret
and with an air of cheerfulness,
uttered three tiny words into
the shadowy gloom –
the secret to Teddy's happiness.

So they caught a train . . .

. . . then a plane . . .

. . . and sailed the whole night through,
with three tiny words for a sad old bear,
three magical words . . .

...we love you.

Other Gullane Children's Books for you to enjoy

Ferdie and the Falling Leaves
Julia Rawlinson
illustrated by
Tiphanie Beeke

Holly's Red Boots
Francesca Chessa

The Lamb-a-roo
Diana Kimpton
illustrated by
Rosalind Beardshaw

Tom's Tree
Gillian Shields
illustrated by
Gemma Raynor

Ten in the Bed
Jane Cabrera

I Love You, Always and Forever
Jonathan Emmett
illustrated by
Daniel Howarth